Contents

2 Taking Off

4 How a Helicopter Flies

6 Choppers vs Planes

8 Different Helicopters

10 Search and Rescue

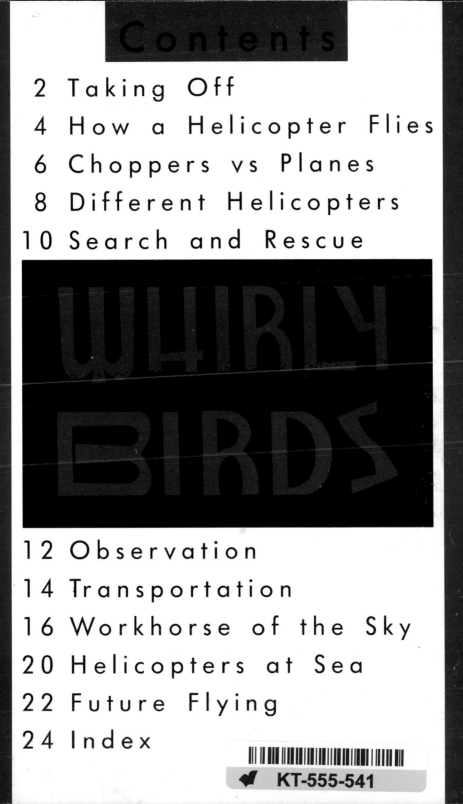

12 Observation

14 Transportation

16 Workhorse of the Sky

20 Helicopters at Sea

22 Future Flying

24 Index

They have been called whirlybirds, choppers, and eggbeaters. The real name for these machines, however, comes from two Greek words: *helix*, meaning spiral, and *pteron*, a wing. We're talking about helicopters, of course, those daredevil machines of the sky. Wherever there's action, a crisis, or a difficult job to do, there will probably be a helicopter on the scene.

The earliest idea for a rotor-powered flying machine was recorded as far back as A.D. 320. This was in a Chinese book with a design for a child's toy consisting of a flying top with feather rotors.

Below right:
Leonardo da Vinci's
helicopter sketch

Later designs included a sketch by the great Italian artist and scientist Leonardo da Vinci in 1483. Da Vinci's "helicopter" had propellers made of starched

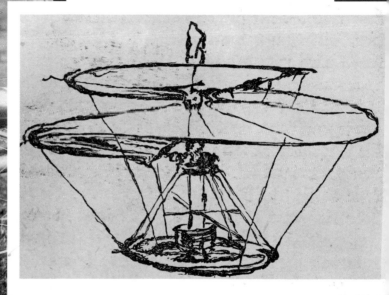

linen. But it wasn't until many centuries later that the first helicopter made it off the ground.

Above: Paul Cornu in the tandem-rotor craft he built in 1907

Taking Off

The main problem in developing a craft that could fly was finding an engine both light enough and powerful enough to drive a heavier-than-air machine. The solution didn't turn up until the invention of the petrol engine at the end of the nineteenth century.

Both fixed-wing planes and helicopters need *lift* to fly. This is produced by the wings. In the case of the helicopter, these are rotary wings, or *blades*. They whirl around in the air, driven by the *rotor*, which in turn is powered by the engine.

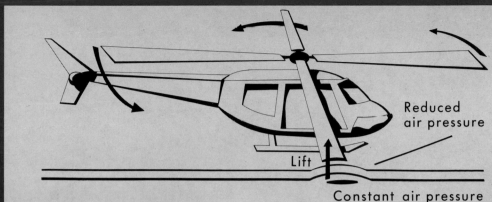

Reduced air pressure

Lift

Constant air pressure

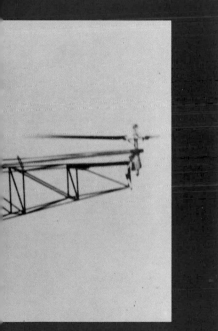

Early helicopter flight by engineer Igor Sikorsky

It is the special shape of the wings (curved on top and flat on the lower surface) which gives the helicopter vertical lift. Air flows at different rates next to the blades, faster over the top of the wing than under it. The slower air exerts greater pressure than the fast air, pushing the blades upwards. This contrast in pressures creates the lift needed by the helicopter.

Choppers vs Planes

Helicopters have many advantages over aeroplanes. They are easier to manoeuvre, being able to fly straight up and down, and even hover.

Unlike fixed-wing planes, they don't need a runway for take-offs or landings. In some cities, there are even *heliports* (airports for helicopters) on top of tall buildings.

Helicopters can also fly safely at low altitudes, in contrast to most planes.

1. COLLECTIVE PITCH LEVER: enables the machine to hover, climb or descend.

2. CONTROL COLUMN OR CYCLIC PITCH CONTROL: causes the machine to fly forward, backward or sideways.

3. RUDDER PEDALS: control direction by swinging the tail around so the helicopter can turn.

4. TORQUE: controls tail rotor. (Torque is the twisting force which spins the aircraft in the opposite direction to the main rotor.) Torque is counteracted by the tail rotor.

However, their flying power has its limitations, too. Strong vibrations which develop at speeds above 320 kph (200 mph) can damage the machine's blades. This means that most helicopters cannot fly as fast as planes.

They also use more fuel to cover the same distance. Helicopters can fly for only two to three hours — or less than 970 km (600 mi) — without refuelling.

Helicopters come in all shapes and sizes. Military attack helicopters are small and light but sturdy. They can fly fast and are very agile.

In contrast, transport helicopters must be big enough to carry cargo or passengers. One of the world's largest helicopters is the Soviet Mil MI-12 *Homer*. It has a span of 67 m (220 ft) and is 37 m (120 ft) long.

The number of blades they have also varies. *Single-rotor* helicopters (which actually have two rotors) are the most common. They have a main rotor on the aircraft body, and another smaller rotor mounted on the tail. This design was developed by Ukrainian-born American engineer Igor Sikorsky, who always test-flew his own machines.

An earl

Twin-rotor helicopters have two main rotors, which turn in opposite directions. This eliminates the need for a tail rotor. They are either *tandem-rotor* craft, where the rotors are at each end of the chopper's body, or *coaxial-rotor* craft, with one rotor above the other in the middle.

One thing all helicopters have in common is the variety of tasks they can perform.

ky helicopter

Tandem-rotor craft

Helicopters are best known for their search and rescue missions. Over the years, they have plucked thousands of people from burning skyscrapers, sinking ships, and rising floodwaters, and rescued stranded mountain climbers and injured skiers.

When a helicopter appears at the scene of an emergency, it hovers above while a sling or harness is lowered. The trapped or injured person is then pulled up and flown to safety.

Choppers are crucial in sea rescues, where the weather may prevent lifeboats from rescuing exhausted swimmers or injured sailors. Amphibious helicopters are watertight and land on floats, while land helicopters are often fitted with inflatable pontoons for emergency landings at sea.

Because they need little landing space, helicopters can land close to the site of a crash, for example, where a plane has come down in mountains or forest. The chopper is often equipped to serve as a flying ambulance, with stretchers and medical equipment. In bad traffic accidents, a helicopter can get an injured person to a hospital much faster than a road ambulance.

Search and Rescue

Helicopters can fly at much lower heights than fixed-wing planes. This makes them ideal for aerial observation work, which could be anything from inspecting power lines to aiding the police.

Using helicopters to fly low along pipelines, railway tracks, and power lines to check for damage is less time-consuming than using ground vehicles.

Police use helicopters to direct patrol cars on the ground to lost people, burglars, or escaped convicts, among other things. Some countries, like the United States, use them to patrol national borders for smugglers and illegal immigrants.

In many cities, commuters who travel to work by car listen out for radio reports warning of traffic jams. These "eye in the sky" broadcasts come from helicopters, which are used to observe traffic flow for any trouble spots such as accidents.

Many radio and television stations rely on helicopters to cover news events from the air. Filming movies from a helicopter also gives audiences a bird's-eye view of the action.

Observation

Travelling to and from heliports on top of downtown buildings saves business executives time spent in traffic jams. Political leaders in many countries travel by chopper for reasons of security and speed. Many pop stars arrive at their concerts in a helicopter to avoid the crowds of fans; and very wealthy people, like the British royal family, have helipads in their back yards!

People who work in hard-to-reach locations also rely on this aircraft as a method of transport. Oil workers on offshore drilling operations use helicopters like buses to get to their daily jobs. They ferry in crews and supplies, landing on helipads on the platforms.

Hydrographers (people who chart seas, lakes, and rivers) are dropped into remote stretches of coastline to help them carry out their surveys more accurately. Many lighthouses are also serviced in this way.

Helicopters are an essential part of the military. They act as flying ambulances and troop transport, carrying personnel and artillery to battle positions. They also fly jeeps, tanks, and other equipment to wherever they are needed.

Helicopter transport can be for fun, too! Heli-skiing, heli-fishing, and rafting are all sports using a helicopter to reach areas of wilderness off the beaten track.

Transportation

Helicopters not only fly in people, supplies, and equipment, but actually do some of the work, too. Some powerful helicopters are used as "flying cranes" to install antennas or huge air conditioners on top of tall buildings, and to erect electricity transmission towers. Helicopters have even been used to put the crosses on church steeples!

These "workhorses of the sky" are used to pour concrete into seemingly unreachable places and put long bridge sections in position.

A single wire rope dangling from the craft can lift a load weighing up to ten tonnes. Large or awkward cargo is carried in a sling underneath.

Helicopters are a big help in the forestry industry, too. Using helicopters to transport logging crews in and out of forests saves companies the expense and wasted space of building roads. They then hover over inaccessible places to pick up felled timber and haul it back to waiting logging trucks.

Workhorse
of the
Sky

When a forest fire breaks out, helicopters play an important role. They fly in fire-fighters with water containers, known as monsoon buckets, and direct operations on the ground. Sometimes the downwash from the rotors can be used to blow the smoke away and help divert the course of the fire.

In Canada, the same technique is used to blow ice and snow off the trees so logging can continue in midwinter.

Rotor downwash is also used in some cases to remove frost from citrus fruit as the helicopter flies over an orchard. Valuable crops like cherries have been saved by blowing raindrops off the fruit.

The most common use of helicopters on the farm, though, is for spraying fertilizers, spreading seeds, and pest control.

On large ranches, choppers help with rounding up cattle and sheep. One helicopter is said to do the work of fifteen ranch hands. The choppers find and transport injured animals as well.

Rounding up wild horses

In some places helicopters are used for capturing wild deer. The helicopters fly low over the ground and shoot nets over the animals, which are then taken back to farms for breeding.

At sea, helicopters are used to spot shoals of fish and direct fishing fleets to them.

Naval helicopters are on the lookout for a different catch. Equipped with sonar detectors, they locate and track submarines, and may be armed with depth charges. These aircraft are attached to a naval ship with facilities for the helicopter to land on deck. During wartime, there is widespread military use of helicopters to observe movements of enemy troops and ships.

Ships other than those in the navy use helicopters, too. Most vessels used for Arctic and Antarctic surveys and exploration carry at least one helicopter. These are involved in ice floe reconnaissance (tracking the movement of icebergs), among other things. Scientists travel by helicopter to remote polar areas when crevasses make the ice almost impassable.

Merchant ships transfer crews and cargo by helicopter, loading and unloading between ship and shore where it's difficult for the ship to dock. In some harbours, helicopters lower harbour pilots onto incoming vessels to direct them into port.

What happens when you cross a helicopter with an aeroplane? You get an *X-wing*! This is a new type of aircraft, which combines the best features of both — the vertical take-off of a helicopter and the speed of a plane.

X-wing

An X-wing looks like a helicopter, but its four broad, stiff rotors act more like wings. It takes off by rotating these wings, though they cannot be tilted. The vehicle relies on the thrust of the engine for forward flight. When the flying speed is fast enough, the wings stop spinning and act like fixed wings. The aircraft can then increase speed up to 850 kph (530 mph).

Future Flying

Another new-look machine is the *tilt-rotor*. This has blades which can be twisted to vary the amount of lift produced, and engines which rotate from horizontal to vertical. Tilt-rotor craft can take off vertically and fly at up to 560 kph (350 mph).

Tilt-rotor

The helicopter is still changing shape. In whatever form, though, it is a vital part of modern life.

Index

agricultural work	18
amphibious helicopters	10
film work	13
flying ambulances	11,15
flying cranes	16
forestry work	16,18
heliports	6
heli-sport	15
military helicopters	8,15
naval helicopters	20
police work	12
rescue helicopters	10
rotor blades	4,8
tilt-rotor craft	23
traffic observation	13
X-wing	22